Favorite Fairy Tales
∼ Told In ∼
GERMANY

Favorite Fairy Tales
~ Told In ~
GERMANY

Retold from the Brothers Grimm

by Virginia Haviland

Illustrated by Diane Paterson

A Beech Tree Paperback Book
New York

First Beech Tree Edition, 1994, published by arrangement with Little, Brown and Co.
Printed in the United States of America

10 9 8 7 6 5 4 3 2 1

Library of Congress Cataloging-in-Publication Data

Kinder - und Hausmärchen. English.
    Favorite fairy tales told in Germany / compiled by Virginia Haviland ;
illustrated by Diane Paterson.
        p.   cm.
    Summary: Seven well-known German tales: The Frog Prince, The Elves and the
Shoemaker, Rapunzel, The Cat and the Mouse in Partnership, Rumpelstiltskin,
Hansel and Gretel, and The Bremen Town Musicians.
    ISBN 0-688-12592-1
    1. Fairy tales — Germany. [1. Fairy tales. 2. Folklore — Germany.]
I. Grimm, Jacob, 1785-1863. II. Grimm, Wilhelm, 1786-1859.   III. Haviland,
Virginia, 1911- 1988. IV. Paterson, Diane, 1946-   ill. V. Title
PZ8. F288   1994
398. 21' 0943 —dc20   93-29706
                                                           CIP
                                                            AC

Minor editorial and style changes have been made in the stories for these new editions.

For Peter

My most omnivorous reader

— V. H.

Contents

The Frog Prince

The Frog Prince

IN THE OLDEN TIME, when wishing was some good, there lived a king whose daughters were all beautiful. But the youngest was loveliest of all. Even the sun, that looked on many things, marveled when it shone upon her face.

Near the King's palace there was a large dark forest, and in the forest, under an old lime tree, was a well. When the day was very hot the youngest Princess used to go into the forest and sit upon the edge of this cool well. When she was tired of doing nothing, she would play with a golden ball, throwing it up into the air and catching it again. This was her favorite game.

Now one day it happened that the ball did not fall back into her hand. It fell to the ground and rolled right into the well. The Princess followed it with her eyes as it sank in the water, but the well was so very deep that she could not see the bottom. Then she began to cry, louder and louder.

As she was crying, someone called out to her, "What is the matter, Princess? Your tears would move even a stone."

When she looked to the spot where the voice was coming from, she saw only a frog lifting its big ugly face out of the water.

"Oh, it's you, is it, old water-splasher? I am crying for my golden ball, which has fallen into the well."

"Be quiet then, and stop crying," answered the

frog. "I know what to do. But what will you give me if I bring back your ball?"

"Whatever you like, you dear old frog," she said. "My clothes, my pearls and diamonds, or even the golden crown upon my head."

The frog answered, "I care not for your clothes, your pearls and diamonds, nor even your golden crown; but if you will let me be your playmate, and sit by you at table, and eat out of your plate, and drink out of your cup, and sleep upon your little bed—if you will promise to do all this, I will go down and fetch your ball."

"Oh, yes," she agreed quickly, "I promise all you ask, if only you will bring my ball back again to me."

To herself, the Princess thought, "What is the silly old frog chattering about? He lives in the well, croaking with his mates. He cannot live with a human being."

As soon as the frog had her promise, he ducked

his head under the water and sank down. After a little while, he came back with the ball in his mouth, and threw it on the grass beside her.

The Princess was full of joy when she saw her pretty toy again. She picked it up and ran off with it.

"Wait! Wait!" cried the frog. "Take me with you. I can't run as fast as you can."

But what was the good of his crying *croak! croak!* as loud as he could? The Princess did not listen to him. She ran home and forgot all about the poor frog. He had to go back to his well again.

The next day, as the Princess was sitting at dinner with the King and all the court, eating from her golden plate, something came flopping up the stairs … *flip, flap … flip, flap.*

Soon there was a small rap on the door and a little voice cried, "Youngest daughter of the King, you must let me in."

The Princess ran to see who it was. When she

opened the door and saw the frog, she shut it again very quickly and went back to the table, for she was afraid.

The King noticed that her heart was beating very fast, and he said, "My child, what is the matter? Is there a giant at the door, wanting to take you away?"

"Oh no!" she said, "It's not a giant, but a horrid frog."

"What does the frog want with you?"

"Oh, Father dear, last night when I was playing by the well in the forest, my golden ball fell into the water. And I cried, and the frog got it out for me. Then, because he insisted on it, I promised that he should be my playmate. I never thought that he would come out of his water, but there he is, and he wants to come in."

Then they heard the frog knock at the door a second time and cry:

Youngest daughter of the King,
Open your door, I beg!
Remember your words of yesterday, and
Open the door, I beg!

The King said, "What you have promised, you must do. Go and let the frog come in."

So she opened the door. The frog hopped in and followed her to her chair. There he sat, and cried, "Lift me up beside you." The Princess was slow about it, till at last the King ordered her to do it.

When the frog was put on the chair, he asked to be placed upon the table. Then he said, "Push your golden plate near me, that we may eat together." She did as he asked, but not happily.

The frog ate a good dinner, but the Princess could not eat a thing. As last he said, "I have eaten enough, and I am tired. Carry me into your bedroom and arrange your bed, so that we may go to sleep."

The Princess began to cry, for she was afraid of the clammy frog, which she hardly dared to touch, and which was now to sleep in her pretty little bed.

But the King grew very angry. He said, "What you have promised, you must now do."

So the Princess picked up the frog with her finger and thumb and carried him upstairs, where she put him in a corner of her room. When she had got into bed, he crept over and said, "I am tired, and I want to sleep as well as you do. Lift me up, or I will tell your father."

Then she became very angry. She picked him up and threw him with all her might against the wall, saying, "Now you may rest, you horrid frog!" But when he fell to the ground, he had changed from a frog into a handsome Prince with kind and beautiful eyes.

The Prince told her that a wicked fairy had turned him into a frog. Nobody could have freed him from the spell but the Princess herself.

Afterward, at her father's wish, the Prince became the husband of the Princess.

When the sun rose on the day after the wedding, a coach drove up. It was drawn by eight milk-white horses with white plumes on their heads and a golden harness. Behind them stood faithful Henry, the Prince's servant, full of joy at his master's freedom. He had brought the coach to carry the young pair back to the Prince's own kingdom. The Prince and his bride rode away, and they lived happily ever after.

The Elves and the Shoemaker

The Elves and the Shoemaker

THERE WAS ONCE a shoemaker who, through no fault of his own, had become poor. Finally he had leather enough left to make only one more pair of shoes.

One night he cut out the shoes which he would sew the next morning. Then he lay down, said his prayers, and fell asleep.

In the morning, after he had said his prayers and was ready to sit down to work, he found a fine pair of shoes standing finished on his table.

He was so astonished he did not know what to think!

He took the shoes in his hand to examine them closely. They were beautifully polished, and so neatly sewn that not one stitch was out of place. They were as good as the work of a master shoe-maker.

Soon a customer came in. He was so pleased with the shoes that he paid much more than the usual price for them, Now the shoemaker had enough money to buy leather for two more pairs of shoes.

The shoemaker cut these out that evening. The next day, full of fresh courage, he was about to go to work. But he did not need to—for when he got to his table, he found the shoes finished!

Buyers were not lacking for these shoes, either. The shoemaker received so much money that he was able to buy leather for four pairs of shoes this time.

Early next morning he found the four pairs finished, beautifully; and so it went on. Whatever he cut out in the evening was finished by morning. The shoemaker was soon making a good living again, and became a well-to-do man.

One evening, not long before Christmas, when he had cut out some shoes as usual, the shoemaker said to his wife, "How would it be if we were to sit up tonight to see who it is that lends us such a good helping hand?"

The wife agreed, and lighted a candle. Then the husband and wife hid themselves in the corner of the room, behind some clothes which were hanging there.

At midnight two little men came in through the window and sat down at the shoemaker's table. They took up the work lying cut out before them and began to stitch, sew, and hammer with their tiny fingers and tiny tools. They did this all so neatly and quickly that the shoemaker could not

believe his eyes. The elves did not stop working till everything stood finished on the table. Then they ran quickly away.

The next day the wife said, "These little elves have made us rich. We are no longer hungry, and we ought to thank them. They run about with so little on—they must be freezing cold. I'll make them little shirts, coats, and trousers. I'll even knit each of them a cap and a pair of stockings, and you shall make them each a pair of shoes."

The husband agreed. By evening, they had all these presents ready. They laid on the table two tiny red suits, finely knit green stockings and caps, and shining pairs of little leather shoes. Then they hid themselves, to see how the elves would receive these.

At midnight the elves came skipping in, and were about to set to work. But instead of finding leather ready, they found the beautiful little clothes.

At first they acted only surprised, but then greatly delighted. As quickly as they could, they put on the little shirts, coats, and trousers, the stockings and caps, and the shoes. They smoothed them down and sang:

Now we're boys so fine and neat,
Why cobble more for others' feet?

They hopped and danced about and leaped over the chairs and tables. Then they ran away through the window. From that time on, they were not seen again in the shoemaker's shop. But the shoemaker did well as long as he lived, and was lucky in everything he undertook.

Rapunzel

Rapunzel

ONCE UPON A TIME a man and his wife were very unhappy because they had no children. They lived in a house with a little window in back which looked into a beautiful garden full of the finest flowers and vegetables. But a high wall surrounded the garden, and no one dared enter—because it belonged to a witch of great power, who was feared by all the world.

One day the woman stood at the window,

31

looking at the vegetables. She saw a bed full of the finest rampion. The leaves looked so fresh and green that she longed to eat them. This desire grew day by day. Just because she knew she couldn't get the rampion, she pined away and became pale and ill.

Her husband grew alarmed and said, "What ails you, my dear wife?"

"Alas," she answered, "if I don't get some rampion to eat from that garden behind the house, I know I shall die."

The man, who loved her dearly, said to himself, "Come. Rather than lose my wife, I shall pick her some rampion, no matter what the cost."

So at dusk he climbed over the wall into the witch's garden, hastily picked a handful of rampion leaves, and took them back to his wife. She made them into a salad, which tasted so good that her longing for the rampion was greater than ever.

Nothing would do but that her husband should

climb over the garden wall again and fetch her some more. So, at dusk, over he went. But when he reached the other side he drew back in terror. There, standing before him, was the old witch.

"How dare you," said she, "climb into my garden like a thief and steal my rampion? You shall suffer for this."

"Oh," he implored, "do pardon me. I had to come. My wife saw your rampion from her window and had such a craving for it that she would certainly have died without it."

Then the witch's anger lessened, and she said, "If it's as you say, you may take as much rampion away with you as you like, but on one condition only. You must give me the child your wife will shortly bring into the world. I will look after it like a mother, and all shall go well with it."

In his fear, the man agreed.

When the child was born, the witch appeared. She gave the baby the name of Rapunzel, which means rampion, and carried it off with her.

Rapunzel grew to be the most beautiful child under the sun; but when she was twelve years old, the witch shut her up in a tower in the middle of a great wood.

This tower had neither stairs nor doors, and only one little window high up in the wall. When the witch wanted to enter the tower, she stood at the foot of it and cried out:

Rapunzel, Rapunzel,
Let down your golden hair.

Rapunzel had wonderful long hair, and it shone like gold. Whenever she heard the witch's voice, she did as she was bade. She unloosed her braids, and let her hair fall down from the window so that the old witch could climb up.

After they had lived like this for a few years, it happened one day that a Prince was riding through the wood and passed by the tower. As he drew near it, he heard someone singing so sweetly that he stopped, spellbound, to listen. It was the lonely Rapunzel, trying to while away the time by letting her sweet voice ring out into the wood.

The Prince longed to see who owned this lovely voice, but he sought in vain for a door in the tower. He rode home, so enchanted by the song he had heard that he returned every day to the wood to listen.

One day, when he was standing out of sight behind a tree, he heard the old witch come to the tower and call out:

Rapunzel, Rapunzel,
Let down your golden hair.

Then he saw Rapunzel let down her braids and the witch climb up.

"So *that's* the ladder, is it?" said the Prince. "I, too, will climb it and try my luck."

On the following day, at dusk, he went to the foot of the tower and cried:

Rapunzel, Rapunzel,
Let down your golden hair.

And as soon as she had let it down, the Prince climbed up.

At first Rapunzel was terribly frightened. She had never seen a man before. But the Prince spoke to her in a kindly way. He told her that his heart had been so touched by her singing that he knew he would have no peace of mind till he had seen her.

Rapunzel began to forget her fear. When the Prince asked her to marry him, she consented at once. For, she thought, he is young and handsome, and I'll certainly be happier with him than with the old witch.

So she put her hand in his and said, "Yes, I will gladly go with you, but how am I to get down out of the tower?"

Then she added, "Every time you come to see me you must bring a skein of silk with you. I will make it into a ladder. When it is ready, I'll climb down, and you shall take me away on your horse."

They arranged that, till the ladder was finished, the Prince was to come to her every evening, because the old witch was with her during the day.

The witch, of course, knew nothing of what was going on, till one day Rapunzel said to her, not thinking, "How is it, good Mother, that you are so much harder to pull up here than the young Prince? He is always with me in a moment."

"Oh, you wicked child!" cried the witch. "What is this I hear? I thought I had you hidden safely from the whole world, and yet you have managed to deceive me."

In her rage, she seized Rapunzel's beautiful hair. She wound it round and round her left hand, picked up a pair of shears, and then, *snip, snap,* off came the golden braids. Worse than this, she took

Rapunzel away from the tower to a wild and lonely place and left her to live in misery.

That very evening, the witch returned and fastened the braids to a hook by the window.

The Prince came and called out:

Rapunzel, Rapunzel,
Let down your golden hair.

And the witch let the braids down, so the Prince could climb up as usual. But instead of his beloved Rapunzel, he found the old witch.

She looked at him with angry and wicked eyes and cried mockingly, "Ah-ha! You came to fetch your lady love, but the pretty bird is no longer singing in her nest. The cat has snatched her away, and is also waiting to scratch out your eyes. Rapunzel is lost to you forever—you will never see her again!"

The Prince was beside himself with grief. In his despair, he jumped right out of the window. He was not killed, but he was blinded by the thorns that were growing where he fell. He wandered sadly through the wood for several years, eating nothing but roots and berries, and weeping for the loss of his lovely Rapunzel.

★　★　★

At last the Prince came to the place where Rapunzel was living. Suddenly he heard a voice which seemed strangely familiar to him. He walked eagerly toward the sound. When he was quite close, Rapunzel knew him and fell on his neck and wept. Two of her tears touched his eyes, and they became clear again. He could see as well as ever.

The Prince led Rapunzel to his kingdom, where they were received with great joy. And there they lived happily ever after.

The Cat and Mouse
in Partnership

The Cat and Mouse
in Partnership

A CAT ONCE MET A MOUSE. He began to seem so fond of her that at last the mouse agreed to keep house together.

"But we must provide for the winter ahead," said the cat, "or we shall go hungry. And you, little mouse, must take care not to go out or you will be caught in a trap."

Following this advice, they bought a pot of fat. They did not know where to keep it for safety, but after much thinking, the cat said, "I know no place where it would be safer than in the church. Nobody would dare steal anything there. We will put it under the altar, and will not touch it till we have no other food."

So the pot was hidden.

But, before long, the cat had a great desire to taste the fat.

He said to the mouse, "Oh, little mouse, my cousin has brought a son into the world and asked me to be godfather. The child is white, with brown spots, and I am to hold him at the font. Let me go out today, and you stay at home to keep house."

"Oh, yes," said the mouse, "by all means, go. And when you have all the good things to eat, remember me. I would gladly have a drop of sweet red christening wine myself."

Now there wasn't a word of truth in the cat's story. The cat had no cousin, and he had not been invited to be a godfather at all. He went straight to

the church, crept to the pot of fat, and began to lick it. He licked and licked the whole top off. Then he took a walk on the housetops and looked about. He stretched himself out in the sun, and wiped his whiskers every time he thought of the pot of fat. It was evening when he went home.

"Oh, there you are at last," said the mouse. "You must have had a merry day."

"Oh, it went pretty well," answered the cat.

"And what name did you give the child?" asked the mouse.

"Top-off," answered the cat.

"Top-off!" cried the mouse. "What a strange name! Is it a common one in your family?"

"What does it matter?" said the cat. "It's no worse than Crumbstealer, as your godchild is called."

Not long after this, the cat was again overcome by his desires.

He said to the mouse, "You must do me a favor

again by looking after the house alone. For the second time I have been asked to be sponsor, and, as the child has a white ring around its neck, I cannot refuse."

The good little mouse was quite ready to consent. The cat stole away behind the town walls to the church and ate half of the pot of fat. "Nothing tastes better," he said, "than what one eats by oneself." He was quite satisfied with his day's work.

When the cat arrived home, the mouse asked what this child had been named.

"Half-gone."

"Half-gone! What is that you say? I have never heard such a name in my life! I don't believe you will find it in the name-day calendar!"

Soon the cat's mouth watered again for the fat.

"Good things always come in threes," he said to the mouse. "Again I am to stand godfather. This child is quite black, with big white paws but not another white hair on its body. Such a thing occurs only once in a few years. You will let me go out again, won't you?"

"Top-off! Half-gone!" said the mouse. "They are such curious names. They set me thinking."

"You sit at home in your dark gray velvet coat," said the cat, "getting your head full of fancies. It all comes of not going out in the daytime."

During the cat's absence, the mouse cleaned and made the house tidy—while the greedy cat ate up all the fat.

"When it's all gone, my mind can be at peace," he said to himself, as he went home late at night, stuffed and satisfied.

The mouse at once asked what name had been given to the third child.

"It won't please you any better than the others," said the cat. "He is called All-gone."

"All-gone!" exclaimed the mouse. "I have never

seen that name in print. All-gone! Whatever can it mean?"

She shook her head, curled herself up, and went to sleep.

★　★　★

From this time on, nobody asked the cat to be godfather.

When winter came and there was no food to be had out of doors, the mouse began to think of their hidden store. "Come, cat," she said, "we will get the pot of fat which we have saved. Won't it taste good, now?"

"Yes, indeed!" answered the cat. "You will enjoy it just as much as putting your tongue out of the window."

They started off to the church. When they got there, they found the fat-pot still in its place, but quite empty.

"Alas," said the mouse. "Now I see it all! You have been some true friend! You ate it all up when you went to be godfather. First Top-off, then Half-gone, then—"

"Hold your tongue," cried the cat. "Another word, and I'll eat you too."

But the poor little mouse had "All-gone" on her lips. Hardly had it come out than the cat made a spring, seized the mouse, and gobbled her up.

Now that's the way of the world, you see.

Rumpelstiltskin

Rumpelstiltskin

THERE WAS ONCE A MILLER who was very poor, but he had a very beautiful daughter.

It happened, one day, that this miller was talking with the King. To make himself seem important, he told the King that he had a daughter who could spin gold out of straw.

The King answered, "That would suit me well. If your daughter is as clever as you say, bring her to my castle tomorrow, so that I may see for myself what she can do."

When the girl was brought to him, he led her into a room that was full of straw. He gave her a wheel and spindle and said, "Now set to work. If by early morning you have not spun this straw to gold, you shall die."

He locked the door and left her alone.

And so the poor miller's daughter sat. For the life of her, she could not think what to do. She had no idea how to spin gold from straw. Her plight was so hopeless that she began to weep.

Then all at once the door opened. In came a little man, who said, "Good evening, Miller's Daughter. Why are you crying?"

"Oh," answered the girl, "I have to spin gold out of straw—and I don't know how to do it."

The little man asked, "What will you give me if I spin it for you?"

"My necklace," answered the girl.

The little man took the necklace. He sat down before the wheel, and— *whirr, whirr, whirr!*—three times round, and the bobbin was full of gold. Then he took up another, and—*whirr, whirr, whirr!*—three times round, and that one was full. So he went on till the morning, when all the straw was spun and all the bobbins were full of gold.

At sunrise, in came the King. When he saw the gold, he was astonished—and very pleased, for he was greedy. He had the miller's daughter taken into another room filled with straw, much bigger than the last. He told her that if she wanted to live she must spin all this in one night.

Again the girl did not know what to do, so she began to cry. The door opened, and the same little man appeared as before. He asked, "What will you give me if I spin all this straw into gold?"

"The ring from my finger," answered the girl.

So the little man took the ring, and began again to send the wheel whirring round.

By the next morning all the straw was spun into glittering gold. The King was happy beyond words. But, as he could never have enough gold, he had the miller's daughter taken into a still larger room full of straw, and said, "This straw, too, you must spin in one night. If you do, you shall be my wife." He thought to himself, "Although she is but a miller's daughter, I am not likely to find anyone richer in the whole world."

As soon as the girl was alone, the little man came for the third time and asked, "What will you give me if I spin this straw for you?"

"I have nothing left to give," answered the girl.

"Then you must promise me the first child you have after you are Queen," said the little man.

"Well, who knows what may happen?" thought the girl. As she could think of nothing else to do, she promised the little man what he demanded. In return, he began to spin, and he spun until all the straw was gold.

In the morning when the King came and found everything done as he wished, he had the wedding held at once, and the miller's pretty daughter became Queen.

★ ★ ★

In a year's time, a beautiful child was born. The

Queen had forgotten all about the little man—until one day he came into her room suddenly and said, "Now give me what you promised me."

The Queen was terrified. She offered the little man all the riches of the kingdom—if only he would leave the child.

But the little man said, "No, I would rather have a baby than all the treasures of the world."

The Queen began to weep, so that the little man felt sorry for her.

"I will give you three days," he said, "and if in that time you cannot guess my name, you must give me the child."

The Queen spent the whole night thinking over all the names she had ever heard. She sent a messenger through the land to ask far and wide for all the names that could be found.

When the little man came next day, she began with Caspar, Melchior, and Balthazar, and she repeated all she knew.

But after each the little man said, "No, that is not my name."

The second day the Queen sent to ask all the neighbors what their servants were called. She told the little man all the most unusual names, saying, "Perhaps you are called Cow-ribs, or Sheep-shanks, or Spider-legs?"

But he answered only, "No, that is not my name."

On the third day the messenger came back and said, "I have not been able to find one single new name. But as I passed through the woods, I came to a high hill. Near it was a little house, and before the house burned a fire. Around the fire danced a funny little man, who hopped on one leg and sang:

Tomorrow at last the child comes in,
For nobody knows I'm Rumpelstiltskin."

You cannot think how pleased the Queen was to hear that name!

Soon the little man himself walked in and asked, "Now, Your Majesty, what is my name?"

At first she asked, "Are you called Jack?"

"No, that is not my name."

"Are you called Harry?"

"No," answered he.

And then she asked, "Perhaps your name is Rumpelstiltskin?"

"The devil told you that! The devil told you that!" shrieked the little man. In his anger he stamped with his right foot so hard that it went into the ground above his knee. Then he seized his left foot with both hands in such a fury that he split in two. And that was the end of him!

Hansel and Gretel

Hansel and Gretel

ONCE UPON A TIME a poor woodcutter with his wife and two children lived at the edge of a large forest. The boy was called Hansel and the girl Gretel. They never had much to eat. Finally, when there was a great famine in their land, the father could not even provide them with daily bread.

One night, when the poor man was tossing about in bed, full of cares and worry, he sighed and said to his wife, who was the children's stepmother, "What is to become of us? How are we to feed our poor children, now that we have nothing even for ourselves?"

"I'll tell you what, Husband," she answered. "Early tomorrow morning we'll take the children out into the thickest part of the wood. There we shall light a fire for them, give them each a piece of bread, and go on to our work, leaving them alone. They won't be able to find their way home, and so we shall be rid of them."

"No, Wife!" said her husband. "That I won't do. How could I find it in my heart to leave my children alone in the wood? The wild beasts would come and tear them to pieces."

"What a fool you are!" she replied. "Then we must all four die of hunger." And she left him no peace until he consented.

"But I cannot help worrying about the poor children," added the husband.

The children were awake, for they had been too hungry to go to sleep. They heard what their stepmother said to their father. Gretel wept bitterly, "Now we're going to die, Hansel."

"No, no, Gretel," said Hansel, "don't cry. I'll find a way to help us."

When the old people had fallen asleep, Hansel got up, put on his little coat, opened the door, and stole out. The moon was shining brightly, and the white pebbles which lay in front of the house glittered like bits of silver. He bent down and filled his pockets with as many as would go in.

Then he went back and whispered to Gretel, "Don't fret, dear little sister. Go to sleep. God will help us." And he lay down in bed again.

At daybreak, even before the sun was up, their stepmother came and woke them. "Get up, you lazybones. We are all going to the forest to fetch wood."

She gave them each a bit of bread and said,

"Here is something to eat, but keep it for your dinner, for you'll get no more."

Gretel put the bread in her apron, for Hansel had the stones in his pockets. Then they all set out together on the way to the forest. When they had walked a little, Hansel stopped and looked back at the house. He did it again and again.

His father noticed this and asked, "Hansel, what are you looking at, and why do you always lag behind? Take care and don't stumble."

"Oh Father," said Hansel, "I am looking at my white kitten. It is sitting on the roof, waving good-by to me."

His stepmother exclaimed, "Little fool! That isn't your kitten, it is the morning sun shining on the chimney."

But Hansel had not been looking at the roof. He had been dropping the little white pebbles on the path.

When they had reached the middle of the forest

their father said, "Now, children, pick up some wood and I'll light a fire to warm you."

Hansel and Gretel gathered twigs and soon made a huge pile. The wood was lighted, and when it blazed up their stepmother said, "Now lie down by the fire and rest yourselves, while we go and cut wood. When we have finished we'll come back to get you."

Hansel and Gretel sat down beside the fire, and at midday ate their little bits of bread. They heard the sound of an ax, so they thought their father was quite near. It was no ax, however, but a branch which was being blown about by the wind. They sat for such a long time that their eyes began to close, and they went fast asleep.

When they awoke, it was dark.

Gretel began to cry, and said, "How will we ever get out of this forest?"

But Hansel comforted her. "Wait," he said, "till the moon rises. Then we'll find our way home."

When the full moon had risen, Hansel took his little sister by the hand. They followed the pebbles, which shone like new pieces of money, and showed them the path. All night long they walked, until at daybreak they found themselves back at their father's house.

When their stepmother answered their knock, she exclaimed, "You naughty children, why did you sleep so long in the wood? We thought you didn't mean to come back." The father was delighted, for his heart had been heavy at leaving them alone.

Soon, however, came another great famine. One night the hungry children heard their stepmother say, "We have eaten everything. The children must go. This time we shall lead them farther into the wood so they cannot find their way out again."

The father's heart was heavy. He thought to himself, "Surely it would be better to share our last crust with our children!" But his wife would not listen.

When the parents were asleep, Hansel again got up to go out and pick up pebbles. Now, however, he found the door locked, so he could not get out. He comforted his little sister by saying, "Don't cry, Gretel. Go to sleep. The good Lord is sure to help us."

In the early morning the woman made the children get up. She gave them each a piece of bread—even smaller than before. On the way to the wood, Hansel crumbled his in his pocket and every few minutes stopped and dropped a crumb to the ground.

"Hansel, why are you stopping to look back?" asked his father.

"I'm looking back at my little dove, which is sitting on the roof waving good-by to me," answered Hansel.

"Little fool, that isn't your dove," said the woman, "it is the morning sun shining on the chimney."

Hansel went on, dropping crumb after crumb until all the bread was gone.

The woman led the children still deeper into the forest, farther than they had ever been before.

After a big fire was lit, she said, "Just sit down here, children, and when you are tired you may sleep for a while. We are going farther on to cut wood. By evening we shall come back for you."

At midday Gretel shared her bread with Hansel, who had scattered his all along the way. Then they fell asleep. The evening passed, but no one came to get the children.

It was quite dark when they awoke. Hansel cheered his sister by saying, "Just wait, Gretel, until the moon rises. Then we shall see the bread crumbs I scattered along the path. They will show us the way home."

But these they could not see, even when the

moon had risen. The thousands of birds that fly about the woods and fields had eaten every crumb.

"Never mind," said Hansel, "we shall find a way out."

The children wandered about the whole night, and the next day also, from morning till evening. But they could not find a path out of the wood. They became very hungry, for they had had nothing to eat but a few berries which they had found growing on the ground. At last they were so tired that they lay down under a tree and fell fast asleep.

On the third morning they were still wandering. Now they felt that if help did not come soon they would perish.

At midday they saw a beautiful little snow-white bird sitting on a branch. It was singing so sweetly that they stood still to listen to it.

When its song was ended, the bird flapped its wings and flew on in front of them. They followed it until they came to a little house, where it lighted on the roof. With delight, Hansel and Gretel noticed that the house was made of gingerbread. And it had a roof of cakes, with windows made of clear sugar.

"Now," said Hansel, "we'll have a real feast! I'll eat a piece of the roof, Gretel, and you can have a bit of the window. It will be good and sweet."

Hansel reached up and broke off a piece of the roof to see how it tasted. Gretel went to a window and began to nibble. At once a polite voice called out from within:

> *Nibble, nibble, little mouse,*
> *Who is nibbling at my house?*

The children answered:

> *The wind, the wind,*
> *The heaven-born wind.*

And they went on eating.

Hansel, who very much liked the taste of the

roof, tore down a big chunk for himself, while Gretel pushed a whole round pane out of the window and sat down to enjoy it.

Suddenly the door opened. An old, old woman leaning on a crutch hobbled out.

Hansel and Gretel were so frightened that they dropped what they had in their hands.

But the old woman only shook her head and said, "Oh, ho, you dear children! Who brought you here? Come in now and stay with me. No harm shall come to you."

She took them both by the hand and led them into the house. There she gave them a delicious dinner of milk and sugared pancakes, with apples and nuts. After they had eaten, she showed them two pretty little white beds all ready for them. When Hansel and Gretel lay down, they felt as if they were in heaven.

Now, although the old woman seemed to be so friendly, she was really a wicked old witch who lay

in wait for children to come by. She had built the house of gingerbread on purpose to lure them to her. Whenever she could get a child into her power, she cooked the child and ate it and had a real feast day. Witches have red eyes, and cannot see far; but like animals, they have a keen sense of smell and know when human beings pass by. When Hansel and Gretel fell into the witch's hands, she had laughed wickedly and said to herself, "I have them now. They shall not escape."

The witch got up early in the morning, before the children were awake. When she saw them both sleeping so peacefully, with their round rosy cheeks, she muttered to herself, "They will make a dainty tidbit." She seized Hansel with her bony hand, and carried him into a chicken coop and barred the door. "You may scream as much as you like. It will do you no good."

She went back to Gretel, shook her awake, and cried, "Get up, you lazybones! Fetch some water and cook something good for your brother. He's locked in the chicken coop, to be fattened. When he's nice and fat, I shall eat him."

Gretel began to cry bitterly, but it was no use. She had to do what the wicked witch commanded.

The best food was now cooked for poor Hansel, but Gretel had only crab shells. Every morning the old woman hobbled out to the yard and cried,

"Hansel, let me feel your finger, so that I can tell if you are getting fat."

But Hansel always held out a bone. The old woman, whose eyes were dim, could not see. Always thinking it was Hansel's finger, she wondered why he fattened so slowly.

When four weeks had passed in this way, the witch lost patience and would wait no longer. "Now, then, Gretel," she called. "Be quick and get some water. Hansel may be fat or thin. I'm going to cook him tomorrow."

Oh, how his poor little sister sobbed as she carried the water! And how the tears streamed down her cheeks! "Dear God, help us now!" she cried. "If only the wild animals in the wood had eaten us, at least we'd have died together."

"Stop crying," said the old witch, "it will do you no good."

Early in the morning Gretel had to go out to fill

the kettle with water and light a fire. "First we'll do some baking," said the old witch. "I have heated the oven and kneaded the dough." She pushed Gretel towards the oven, from which flames were shooting. "Creep in and see if it is hot enough for the bread." She intended, when she had Gretel in the oven, to close the door and roast her so that she might eat her, too.

But Gretel saw what the witch had in mind and said, "How do I get in?"

"You silly goose," cried the witch, "the opening is big enough. See, I could get in myself." She crawled over and stuck her head into the oven. Gretel gave her a big shove and pushed her right in! Then Gretel closed the door and bolted it.

How the witch yelled! It was quite horrible to hear. But Gretel fled—and left the wicked witch to perish.

★ ★ ★

Gretel ran as fast as she could to the coop. She opened the door, and cried, "Hansel, we are saved! The old witch is dead!"

Hansel sprang like a bird out of an opened cage. The children fell on each other, kissed one another, and danced about for joy. As they had nothing more to fear, they went into the witch's house, and found, in every corner of the room, chests filled with pearls and precious stones.

"These are even better than pebbles," said Hansel, and crammed his pockets full.

"I must take some home with me, too," said Gretel, and filled her apron.

"But now we must leave this haunted wood," said Hansel.

On their way out, they came to a big lake. "We cannot get over this," said Hansel. "I see no stepping stones, and no bridge of any kind."

"There is no ferry boat, either," answered Gretel. "But look, there is a white duck swimming. It will help us over, if we ask." So she called out,

No boat, no bridge—alack, alack;
Please, little duck, take us on your back!

The duck swam toward them. Hansel got on its back and told Gretel to sit beside him. "No," answered Gretel, "it would be too heavy a load for the little duck. It must take us over in turn."

The good bird did this. When the children had got over safely and had walked for a while, the wood seemed to become more and more familiar.

At last they saw their father's house in the distance. They began to run. When they reached the house, they rushed inside to throw their arms around their father's neck. The poor man wept for joy, for he had not had a single happy moment since he had left them in the wood. In the meantime his wife had died.

Gretel shook out her apron and scattered pearls

and precious stones all over the floor. Hansel drew more handfuls of jewels out of his pockets. So, at last, all their troubles came to an end, and they lived together happily ever afterward.

The Bremen Town
Musicians

The Bremen Town Musicians

O NCE UPON A TIME a man had a donkey, which for many years had faithfully carried his grain to the mill. At last, however, the animal's strength began to fail, and he was no longer of any use for work. His master then began to think about getting rid of him. The donkey felt there was something in the air, so he ran away—down the road to Bremen. There, he thought, he could become a town musician.

When he had gone a little way, he found a dog who lay panting on the road as though he had run himself off his legs.

"Well, why are you panting so, Growler?" asked the donkey.

"Ah," answered the dog, "just because I am old, and every day I get weaker. Also, because I can no longer keep up with the other dogs, my master wanted to kill me. So I ran away. But now, how am I to earn my bread?"

"Do you know what?" said the donkey. "I am going to Bremen. There I shall become a town musician. Come with me and take your part in the music. I shall play the lute, and you shall beat the kettledrum."

The dog agreed, and they went on.

A short time after, they came upon a cat, sitting in the road with a face as long as a wet week.

"Well, what has been bothering you, Whiskers?" asked the donkey.

"Who can be cheerful when his neck is in danger?" said the cat. "I am getting old, and my teeth are dull. I prefer to sit by the stove and purr instead of hunting around after mice. Just because of this, my mistress wanted to drown me. I ran away, but now I don't know what is to become of me."

"Come with us to Bremen," said the donkey. "You are a great hand at serenading. You can become a town musician."

The cat agreed, and joined them.

Next, the three passed by a yard where a cock was sitting on the gate, crowing with all its might.

"Your crowing goes through and through one," said the donkey. "What's the matter?"

"Why—because Sunday visitors are coming tomorrow, the mistress ordered the cook to make me into soup! Now I am crowing with all my might while I have the chance."

"Come along, Redcomb," said the donkey.

"We're going to Bremen. You'll find a much better life there. You have a strong voice. When we make music together, it will be good."

The cock agreed, and they all four went off together.

They could not, however, reach the town in one day. By evening they arrived at a wood, where they decided to spend the night.

The donkey and the dog lay down under a big tree. The cat and the cock settled themselves in the branches. The cock flew right up to the top, which was the safest place for him.

Before going to sleep, the cock looked around once more on every side. Suddenly he saw a light burning in the distance. He called out, "There must be a house not far off, for I see a light."

"Very well," said the donkey, "let us set out and make our way to it, for we have little comfort here."

The dog thought, too, that some bones or meat would be just the thing for him, so they set off toward the light. They soon saw it shining more clearly and getting bigger and bigger, till they reached a robber's den all lighted up. The donkey, being the tallest, went up to the window and looked in.

"What do you see, Old Donkey?" asked the cock.

"What do I see?" answered the donkey. "Why, a table spread with delicious food and drink, and robbers seated at it enjoying themselves."

"That would just suit us," said the cock.

"Yes—if only we were there," answered the donkey.

The animals began to think about how they might drive the robbers out.

At last they hit upon a plan: The donkey was to put his forefeet on the window sill. The dog was to jump on his back. The cat would climb up on top of the hound, and last of all the cock was to fly up and perch on the cat's head.

So that was done, and at a given signal they all

began to perform. The donkey brayed, the dog barked, the cat mewed, and the cock crowed. Then they dashed through the window, shattering the glass.

The robbers fled at this terrible noise. They thought that nothing less than a demon was coming, and ran into the wood in the greatest alarm.

The four animals now sat down at the table. They helped themselves and ate as though they had been starving for weeks. When they had finished, they put out the lights and looked for sleeping places, each choosing one that suited its own nature and taste.

The donkey lay down outside, the dog behind the door, the cat on the hearth near the warm ashes, and the cock flew up to the rafters. As they were tired from their long journey, they soon went to sleep.

When midnight was past, and the robbers saw from a distance that the light was no longer

burning and that all seemed quiet, the chief said, "We ought not to have been scared so easily."

He ordered one of the robbers to go back to examine the house.

The robbers found everything quiet, and went on into the kitchen to kindle a light. Taking the cat's glowing, fiery eyes for live coals, he held a match close to them so as to light it. But the cat would stand no nonsense. It flew at his face, spitting and scratching. The man was terribly frightened and ran away.

He tried to get out by the back door, but the dog, who was lying there, jumped up and bit his leg. As the man ran on across the yard, the donkey gave him a good sound kick with his hind legs. The cock, who had been awakened by the noise and felt quite fresh and gay, cried out from his perch, *Cock-a-doodle-doo!*

Thereupon, the robber ran back as fast as he could to his chief, and said, "There is a horrible witch in the house, who breathed on me and scratched me with her long fingers. Behind the door there stands a man with a knife, who stabbed me. In the yard lies a black monster, who hit me with a club. And upon the roof the judge is seated, and he called out 'Bring the rogue here!' So I ran away, as fast as I could."

From that time on, the robbers dared not go near the house, and the four Bremen musicians were so pleased with it that they never wished to leave.

About This Series

I N RECENT DECADES, folk tales and fairy tales from all corners of the earth have been made available in a variety of handsome collections and in lavishly illustrated picture books. But in the 1950s, such a rich selection was not yet available. The classic fairy and folk tales were most often found in cumbersome books with small print and few illustrations. Helen Jones, then children's book editor at Little, Brown and Company, accepted a proposal from a Boston librarian for an ambitious series with a simple goal — to put an international selection of stories into the hands of children. The tales would be published in slim volumes, with wide margins and ample leading, and illustrated by a cast of contemporary artists. The result was a unique series of books intended for children to read by themselves — the Favorite Fairy Tales series. Available only in hardcover for many years, the books have now been reissued in paperbacks that feature new illustrations and covers.

The series embraces the stories of sixteen different countries: Czechoslovakia, Denmark, England, India,

France, Italy, Ireland, Germany, Greece, Japan, Scotland, Norway, Poland, Sweden, Spain, and Russia. Some of these stories may seem violent or fantastical to our modern sensibilities, yet they often reflect the deepest yearnings and imaginings of the human mind and heart.

Virginia Haviland traveled abroad frequently and was able to draw on librarians, storytellers, and writers in countries as far away as Japan to help make her selections. But she was also an avid researcher with a keen interest in rare books, and most of the stories she included in the series were found through a diligent search of old collections. Ms. Haviland was associated with the Boston Public Library for nearly thirty years — as a children's and branch librarian, and eventually as Readers Advisor to Children. She reviewed for *The Horn Book Magazine* for almost thirty years and in 1963 was named Head of the Children's Book Section of the Library of Congress. Ms. Haviland remained with the Library of Congress for nearly twenty years, and wr[...] children's literature throughou[...] 1988.